Rice and Beans

Written by Wiley Blevins
Illustrated by Mattia Cerato

RED CHAIR PRESS

Please visit our website at www.redchairpress.com.
Find a free catalog of all our high-quality products for young readers.

Rice and Beans
Publisher's Cataloging-In-Publication Data
(Prepared by The Donohue Group, Inc.)

Blevins, Wiley.
Rice and beans / written by Wiley Blevins ; illustrated by Mattia Cerato.
p. : col. ill. ; cm. -- (Family snaps)
Summary: A young girl adopted from China sees that her hair and skin color are different from that of her parents. She finds, however, that there's much more to making a family than sharing red hair and freckles.
Interest age level: 005-008.
Issued also as an ebook.
ISBN: 978-1-939656-00-1 (lib. binding/hardcover)
ISBN: 978-1-939656-63-6 (pbk.)
ISBN: 978-1-939656-01-8 (eBk)
1. Adopted children--Juvenile fiction. 2. Individual differences--Juvenile fiction. 3. Identity (Psychology)--Juvenile fiction. 4. Families--Juvenile fiction. 5. Adoption--Fiction. 6. Identity--Fiction. 7. Families--Fiction. I. Cerato, Mattia. II. Title.
PZ7.B618652 Ri 2014

[E]   2013956105

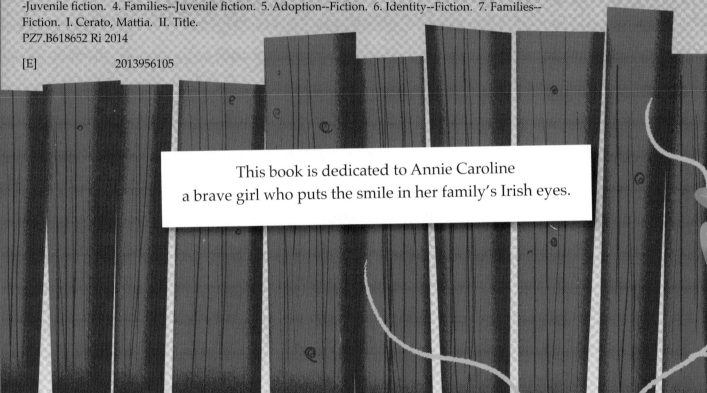

This book is dedicated to Annie Caroline
a brave girl who puts the smile in her family's Irish eyes.

First published by:
Red Chair Press LLC   PO Box 333   South Egremont, MA 01258-0333

Printed in the United States of America

1 2 3 4 5 18 17 16 15 14

Mom said she dreamed of having a girl.

Just like me.

Dad said he wanted me more than turnips.

That's his favorite food. Ick!

My hair is black.

My eyes are black, too.

My **mom** and **dad** have red hair.

And skin the color of vanilla ice cream.

I was born in a place far away.

A place where people say "nee-hou" instead of "hello."

A place where they eat pork dumplings and rice.

Lots and lots of rice.

Now I eat brown beans and cornbread.

Lots and lots of cornbread.

Mom and Dad flew in a plane to get me.

Then we flew home together.

"You cried all the way home," said Dad.

I'm older now. I don't cry much **anymore.**

When we go shopping, people stare.

"Why don't you look like your mom and dad?"

asked a little girl.

I tell her I'm **adopted.**

That means I have a **birth mom**
and a **forever mom.**

My birth mom loved me. But she couldn't take
care of me. She had to let me go.

My forever mom loves me, too.

She says she'll never let me go.

Even when I'm fifty.

I love my dad, too.

He thinks he's the greatest dad ever.

He even has a t-shirt that says so!

My best friend is Anna.

Everyone in her family looks alike.

Even her cat.

Sometimes people think Anna is her sister.

I wouldn't like that.

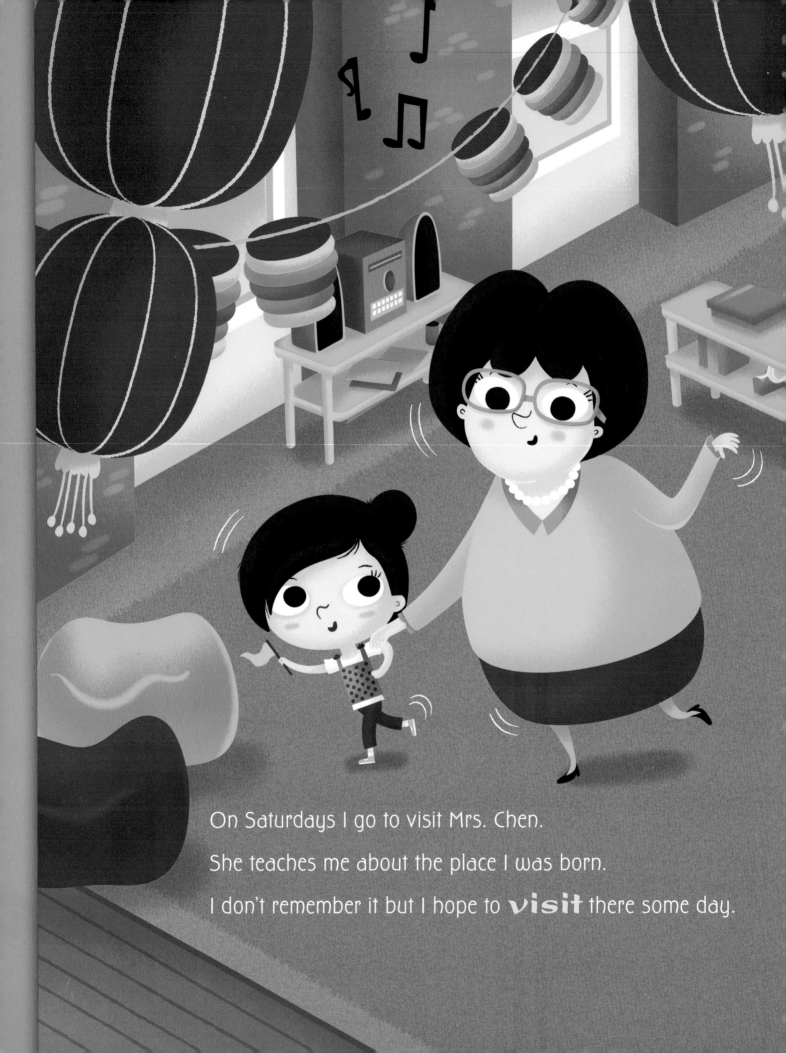

On Saturdays I go to visit Mrs. Chen.

She teaches me about the place I was born.

I don't remember it but I hope to **visit** there some day.

Mrs. Chen teaches me the dragon dance.

She teaches me how to say words in Chinese.

She teaches me how to make **mooncakes.**

I need to learn these things.

Soon, we will have a big parade.

It will be the Chinese New Year!

I will be part of the dragon in the parade.

Mom and Dad are **excited**

to see me in it.

On the day of the parade, Mom dresses me in red.

It is the color of **happiness.**

I join my friends Ling and Han.

We get in place under the big dragon.

Han is under the dragon's head.

The drums beat.

Boom-boom-bang.

The dragon's head goes **up.**

Han goes **down.**

I **peek** out to see my mom and dad.

I spot them in the crowd.

It's easy. I can see their

bright red hair.

They wave and smile.

After the parade we all go to my house.

Mom shows me how to make rice.

I try, but it's a little **too** sticky.

Dad scoops a big lump on his plate.

Mom pours brown beans on top.

"Brown beans and rice are a perfect mix," Dad says.

Then he smiles at *Mom and me.*

Mrs. Chen passes out the mooncakes.

They are filled with yummy jam.

The moon is a Chinese symbol.

It stands for families sticking together.

The mooncakes have little marks on them.

The marks mean "happy life."

I give my mom and dad a mooncake.

Then I hug them.

With them I know I will have a happy life.

We might not look alike.

But we have love.

And love is the glue that sticks us together.

Now if only I could get
my rice less sticky!